Gardening with Sara and Tommy

Dagmar Stam and Francine Oomen

WHITECAP BOOKS
Vancouver/Toronto

Who eats all the strawberries? The birds or you? And who can grow the biggest pumpkin in your family?

In this book Sara and Tommy show you how to grow vegetables, fruit, and flowers yourself. Then your mom and dad won't have to go to the supermarket or flower shop so often. Home-grown fruit and vegetables also taste much fresher and more delicious.

If you don't have a garden you can plant seeds in flower pots or trays. The plants will grow well, although they'll be a little smaller.

Before you start put on your old clothes. Good gardeners know they'll get their hands dirty!

Printed and bound in Singapore.

Canadian Cataloguing in Publication Data

Stam, Dagmar.
  Gardening with Sara and Tommy
  Translation of: Tuinieren met Saartje en Tommie.
  ISBN 1-55110-299-4

  1. Gardening—Juvenile literature.
  I. Oomen, Francine. II. Title.

SB457.S72 1995   j635   C94-910955-X

You will need:

basket

rake

gardening gloves

trowel

ame tags

stakes and string

hoe

spade

watering can

flower pots

seed packets

potting soil

Pumpkins

Sow: May / Harvest: September

The pumpkin is one of the most popular—and easy—vegetables to grow. Just remember to give it lots of room because the plant will become very large!

Buy a packet of seeds and sow them indoors in pots. In about 2 weeks the seeds will sprout. Keep them well watered. The first week in June you can move the plants outside. Plant them in a sunny spot and water them often. The plants will grow and grow…. After a while large yellow flowers will appear. The pumpkins will grow from these. If you are growing them to eat, don't let the pumpkins get too big because they will have less flavor.

Tomatoes

Sow: early March / Harvest: end of June

Tomatoes must be sown indoors. Fill small plastic pots with potting soil. Lay 2 seeds on top of each pot and cover them lightly with soil.

Place the pots in a sunny spot and water them daily. If two plants sprout, remove the weaker one.

At the end of May you can plant them outside. Cut the pot or tip it to remove all the soil with the tomato plant.

Tomatoes grow best in a sheltered, sunny spot. Push a stake into the ground beside each plant. As the plant grows, tie it to the stake so it won't fall over. You will have to remove side shoots or you won't get as many tomatoes. The shoots grow between the main stem and the side branches. If a side branch has four fruits, break off the growing tip or the branch will get too heavy. Pick the tomatoes once they have turned a rich red all over.

Do you know what's delicious? Tomato wedges sprinkled with sugar!

Sweet Peas

Sow: May / Bloom: August to September

Sweet pea flowers come in all colors and smell divine. They're beautiful in a vase, too. Sow the seeds outdoors in a sunny place. When the plants are 10 cm (4 inches) high, you will need to tie them up.

You can tie them in different ways: use wire netting or strings tied between posts, or even a branch stuck into the ground. If you have wire, you can make flowered arches!

Compost

To grow healthy plants, you must provide food for them. Compost is a natural plant food you can make yourself.

Compost is made of garden and kitchen waste, such as cores, peels, and wilted or rotten fruits and vegetables. Washed, crushed eggshells can be added, but never any meats or bones. A compost heap can be started in a back corner of your garden.

Push a pole about a metre (3 feet) long into the ground. Place a layer of twigs around the pole. Put a layer of kitchen waste or garden clippings on top, then a layer of soil. Next add a layer of lime, which can be bought at a gardening centre.

Continue to build layers in this way. When the compost pile is as high as the pole, pull it out. That will let air into the heap, so it rots more quickly. In 6 months, it will have turned into beautiful, crumbly earth! Sprinkle your compost around the garden each spring, and your plants will grow big and strong.

= twigs   = lime

= wastes   = soil

Rhubarb

Plant: Fall / Harvest: June

Rhubarb is an easy plant to grow, and it can become surprisingly big.

Ask someone who has rhubarb plants if you may have a piece. This needs to be done between October and March, when the plant is having its winter rest.

With a spade, carefully dig out a root with at least one knob (growth bud). Plant the cutting in your garden. Rhubarb likes lots of compost and manure in the soil. Don't harvest it until the second year, when the plant will be big and healthy. Always let rhubarb have its second birthday!

Break the stalks off by hand. The leaves can be added to your compost, but never eat them because they are poisonous.

You can make a simple and delicious dessert with rhubarb. Steam the chopped stems in a little water with sugar for 10 minutes. Serve with yogurt.

Happy eating!

Potatoes

Plant: May / Harvest: in 100 days

Look in the potato sack for potatoes with roots, or buy some at the gardening centre. Clean off the excess dirt. Dig a trench about 10 cm (4 inches) deep. Lay the potatoes inside, about 40 cm (16 inches) apart, and cover with soil.

Soon you will see a circle of leaves sprout up. When the plants are about 20 cm (8 inches) high, feed them with compost or manure. Pile extra soil around the plants because potatoes grow underground and need to stay well covered. Potatoes that are exposed above ground become green and poisonous.

One hundred days after planting, you can dig up your new potatoes!

Radishes

Sow: from April on / Harvest: in 3 weeks

Radishes are easy plants and grow very quickly. Just 3 weeks after you plant seeds, they'll be ready to eat! You can buy different varieties of radish to try.

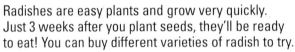

Sow the seeds in well-raked earth, not too deep and not too close to each other. Water well, especially in dry weather. If you plant new seeds every week you'll always have fresh radishes. Don't leave them in the ground too long or they won't taste good. You can have fun with your radishes, too! Try decorating your salad with radish mice, as shown here.

All the Little Beasties!

dung beetle

sow bug (or wood louse)

Both above and under the ground live a great many kinds of animals. Some are so small you cannot see them. They are called micro-organisms. The bigger animals you already know well. They all play important parts in the cycle of nature and all, big and small, are useful. So, don't ever use poisons in your garden.

ant

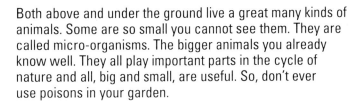
spider

centipede

earwig

snail

earthworm

The cycle of nature means that everything needs every other thing.

A rabbit eats lettuce. Its droppings, and the rabbit too, after it dies, disappear into the ground. The micro-organisms in the ground digest the droppings and bones of the rabbit. The soil they make from these provides food for new lettuce plants to grow, with help from the weather.

Carrots

Sow: early April / Harvest: from July on

First you need to remove all the weeds from your carrot patch. Dig up the soil, then rake it neatly. Pull your rake handle along the ground to make a trench about 2 cm (1 inch) deep. Sow the seeds in the trench and cover them with a thin layer of soil. In 2 weeks the plants will sprout.

When they are 5 cm (2 inches) high you will have to thin them out. Leave about 5 cm (2 inches) between each plant and remove the rest. In about 3 months the carrots will be ready to harvest. If you have more than you can use right away, you can store them in a box filled with sandbox sand. They will stay fresh in the sand for at least another 2 months.

Beans

Sow: mid-May / Harvest: mid-July

Bush beans grow close to the ground.
String beans are climbing plants.
To grow these, you'll need some
long stakes and string to make a
climbing frame for the beans. Look
at the pictures to see how to make
different kinds of frames. Push the
stakes firmly into the ground so they
don't fall out.

Plant six beans for every stake. Wait for dry, sunny
weather. If you sow when it's raining, snails will eat
the beans! In a few days the plants will begin to
show above ground. In 2 months you can pick
your first beans.

Strawberries

Plant: August / Harvest: the next year in June

Ask someone who has strawberry plants if you may have some shoots. Shoots are young plants that grow out from the mother plant. You can break or cut them off carefully. Strawberry plants can also be bought from a gardening centre.

Plant the roots in the soil. Give them extra water for the first two weeks.

The following year, in June, your strawberries will be ready to eat. As they begin to ripen you can lay straw underneath to keep them from rotting.

It's a good idea to place a net over the plants, because birds love strawberries as much as you do!

Stop Thief!

Stop thief! Hey, rabbit! Where are you going with my carrots?

Animals are usually useful. But sometimes they can be pesky robbers. Watch out!

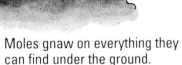

Moles gnaw on everything they can find under the ground. They can be caught with traps.

The slippery slug is mad about young plants. Place a saucer of beer in your garden. The slugs will crawl in and drown.

Birds are crazy about summer fruit. Hang nets over your plants to keep the birds away.

Wire netting will protect your vegetable garden from rabbits. Push the wire into the ground so they can't dig underneath.

Aphids love to eat anything green. But ladybugs just love to eat aphids! Make sure you have some ladybugs in your garden.

Little root flies damage carrots. Spray them with a mixture of soapy water.

Poppies

Sow: April / Bloom: June to September

Did you think that there was just one type of poppy? In fact, there are many!

Sow poppies in moist soil in a sunny spot. In about 2 months the first flowers will appear.

As the flowers finish blooming, the seed heads will swell. Pick a dry seed head—it rattles! If you pull off its lid, its seeds will fall out and sow themselves.

Sunflowers

Sow: March / Bloom: July

Plant two seeds in a small plastic pot filled with potting soil. Set them in a sunny place. If both seeds in a pot sprout, remove the weaker one. At the end of May you can remove the plants from their pots and plant them outside.

Sunflowers love sun and water. They can easily grow as high as 2 metres (7 feet). Mice and birds love sunflower seeds—and you can eat them too!

If you cut off the ripe flowers and dry them, the birds can enjoy a treat in the winter. Be careful to save some seeds to plant next year!

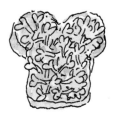

Garden Cress

Sow: indoors, any time / Harvest: in 1 week

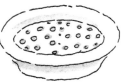

saucer with wet cotton balls

garden cress seeds

after 3 days…

after 7 days, ready to eat!

Garden cress can be sown indoors or outdoors. It grows very fast. You can grow garden cress in an eggcup with a cotton ball, or in an empty, painted eggshell. Try a larger container and set toy animals in it to graze. If you sow your seeds outside, you can spell your name! Garden cress is delicious in a cheese sandwich.

Weeds?!

stinging nettle
Delicious in soup!

Weeds can be very pretty —and some are tasty, too! The annoying thing about weeds is that they always grow where they aren't wanted. They take light and food away from the plants that you want to grow. So you have to get rid of them. You can remove them by hand, or with a spade or a hoe.

dandelion

grasses

nipplewort

creeping buttercup

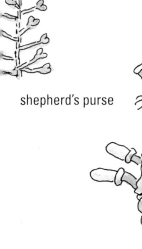

shepherd's purse

chickweed
Great in salads.